WHEN I WAS ALONE

WANDERING TALES

ROHAN KARTIKEYA V

Made with ❤ on the Notion Press Platform
www.notionpress.com

I dedicate this book to a fallen soldier, who is an expert in English literature, My Grandfather. He is and always will be, my English teacher.

Contents

Preface

It was almost 6 years ago when me and my friend thought "Hey what we do if we were alone!" We would talk about hours on end. The day I decided to write books, was the the vary day this idea of a book came to light. So without further ado I present you:

WHEN I WAS ALONE

Prologue

Main Characters

Aditya

Hi! I am Aditya! I am adventurous and love seeking new quests. I also love video games!

Mia

Hi! I am Mia! I am skilled at what I do! I love reading story books in my free time!

Lyla (Book 2)

Hi! I am Lyla! I love animals.

(Book 3 pre)

Mahesh

Hi! I am Mahesh! I am skilled at what I do (not sports.)!! #Topper_of_class

Mukesh

Hi! I am Mukesh! I am rebellious! I love meddling with ancient objects in my free time! (Not really.)

ONE

BOOK 1, WHEN I WAS ALONE

Aditya woke up to an eerie silence, the town eerily quiet. Confusion furrowed his brow as he walked down the empty streets, peering into deserted homes. "Hello?" he called, his voice echoing, but there was no response. It was as if the world had pressed pause on life.

As the day unfolded, Aditya checked every corner of the town. No one was around. No friends, no neighbors.

The playgrounds and schools stood still, void of laughter and chatter. He wandered into the stores, finding untouched snacks and games, waiting for someone to claim them.

In the electronics store, he eyed the shiny PS5. A grin crossed his face as he thought, "Why not?" Aditya grabbed the console and some games, deciding it was time to indulge in a day of play, unrestricted by rules.

Hours passed as he raced virtual cars and battled imaginary monsters. He raided the candy store, munching on snacks he had always wanted to try. Yet, an unsettling thought lingered. Where was everyone? Why was he alone in this silent town?

As night fell, Aditya strolled through the quiet streets, the glow of the console reflecting in his eyes.

He reached the town square, where he found a stray cat. "Hey there, little guy," he said, his loneliness making him seek companionship in

unexpected places. The cat, indifferent to his presence, stared. The next day, Aditya's sense of solitude grew with the sun rising again on the deserted town. "Where did everyone go?" he wondered aloud. Passing the park, he noticed abandoned swings swaying gently in the breeze.

Turning a corner, he encountered a group of dogs in the square. "Hey, buddies, where did everyone vanish to?" he asked, half-expecting them to respond. The dogs wagged their tails, sniffing curiously at the strange human.

Aditya continued his search, encountering a group of cows grazing on the outskirts. "You guys must be wondering where everyone is, too, huh?" he mused, chuckling at the situation's absurdity. The cows stared back, indifferent to his musings.

Still clutching the PS5 controller, Aditya realized that in this newfound solitude, the animals had become his silent companions. Once bustling with human life, the town had transformed into a canvas where he played his games, whispered his thoughts to the wind, and wondered if the animals noticed his presence.

As the sun set again, Aditya sat in the town square, surrounded by dogs, cats, and even a curious raccoon. "Guess it's just us now," he said, gazing at the stars above. The animals, in their silent wisdom, seemed to accept his company in this new, quiet world.

TWO
THOUGHTS?

Aditya's thoughts drifted to the people who once filled these streets with life. Where had they gone? Were they somewhere watching the same stars, pondering the emptiness of their towns? In the quiet, Aditya realized he wasn't truly alone. The animals, each with their unique presence, became his silent confidants. The dogs lay beside him, their warm bodies offering a sense of camaraderie. Cats perched on ledges, observing the night with a mysterious aloofness. The raccoon, always curious, inspected the remnants of Aditya's abandoned snacks. As the night deepened, Aditya and his animal companions developed a silent understanding. He wasn't just a lone human; he was part of this new, harmonious ecosystem. They shared the stillness of the night, finding solace in each other's company.

Days turned into weeks, and Aditya's routine became intertwined with the rhythms of nature. He explored the town by day, sometimes engaging in playful antics with the animals. The dogs chased imaginary creatures, and the raccoon joined Aditya in playful games of hide-and-seek.

Nights were spent in the town square, under the vast expanse of stars. Aditya, sitting on a park bench, strummed a tune on an abandoned guitar he had found. The animals gathered around, listening to the melody as if it were a lullaby for a world that had fallen asleep.

One evening, as Aditya played his guitar, he noticed a group of fireflies dancing in the air. Their tiny lights flickered, creating a magical aura around the square. It was a sight that he might have overlooked in the busyness of human life.

THREE

BEAUTY AND SIMPLICITY

Aditya discovered simplicity's beauty as the days melded into a seamless pattern. No schedules, no expectations, the quiet companionship of animals and the serenity of the deserted town.

As the first light painted the sky one morning, Aditya stood on a hill overlooking the town. The world stretched before him, a canvas of untamed beauty. He realized that perhaps the disappearance of the human world had given rise to a different kind of civilization where the connection between species was silent yet profound.

Aditya ventured into the day with a renewed sense of purpose, accompanied by his animal friends. The world without people had become a sanctuary, a place where the language of nature spoke louder than the chaos of human existence. As they wandered through the quiet town, Aditya and his companions embraced the simplicity of a life where every moment was a silent celebration of fact.

As Aditya and his animal companions continued to explore the silent town, they stumbled upon a neglected community garden. Wildflowers burst forth in vibrant hues, reclaiming the once-manicured beds. Butterflies danced around the blossoms, and bees hummed a gentle melody as they gathered nectar.

Aditya, captivated by the beauty, decided to tend to the garden. He found gardening tools in a shed, and with each careful stroke, he nurtured the once-forgotten plants. The animals, curious and observant, watched him

with keen interest. The garden transformed into a riot of colors and fragrances as days passed.

In the evenings, the town square became a gathering place. Aditya and the animals, now a harmonious community, enjoyed shared moments of calm. The dogs sprawled contentedly, the cats nestled in cozy corners, and the raccoon occasionally brought tiny treasures, shiny pebbles or a fallen leaf as if participating in the communal exchange.

Aditya discovered an abandoned art studio, where canvases and paintbrushes waited patiently for creative hands. Inspired by the surrounding beauty, he began to paint the changing landscapes of the town, capturing the essence of its quiet transformation. His paintings adorned the walls, telling a silent story of a world that had found its own rhythm.

One day, while exploring an old music store, Aditya uncovered a piano hidden beneath dusty sheet. As his fingers danced on the keys, a melody filled the air. The animals, drawn by the enchanting music, gathered around. The notes became a shared language, a symphony of connection that transcended the silence.

A sense of purpose and fulfillment settled within Aditya. The town, once desolate, now echoed with the sounds of life he had helped revive. Yet, a lingering question remained in his mind: Was there a purpose to this newfound existence, or was it simply a beautiful interlude in the tapestry of time?

FOUR

UNDERSTOOD STILLNESS

One evening, as the sun dipped below the horizon, casting long shadows across the town, Aditya stood on the hill once more. The view, now adorned with the setting sun's colors, stirred a quiet contemplation within him.

Aditya felt a subtle shift in the air in that moment of reflection. It was as if the universe itself responded to his musings. The sky, painted in hues of oranges and purples, seemed to hold secrets waiting to be unraveled.

As the night enveloped the town, Aditya gathered his animal companions for a silent vigil under the starlit sky. The universe, with its cosmic ballet, offered no answers, only the beauty of its mysteries.

And so, with a heart full of gratitude and a mind teeming with wonder, Aditya embraced the enigma of his existence. The story of a world without people unfolded with each passing day, a tale woven with threads of connection, creativity, and the profound simplicity of life in the company of silent companions.

Days turned into a rhythm in Aditya's quiet town. The garden he cared for grew colorful, attracting butterflies and the gentle hum of bees. His animal friends stuck close, some joining him on explorations.

Aditya discovered a forgotten bookstore. Books filled with stories and poems waited on dusty shelves. Every night, he read aloud to the animals, creating a cozy bond in the hushed evenings.

One day, he found an old observatory. Climbing to the top, he looked through the telescope at the stars. The silent beauty of the night sky sparked a sense of purpose in Aditya beyond the simple joys of the garden and the piano.

The animals, too, changed. Dogs followed him like loyal companions, cats curled up beside him, and the raccoon kept bringing its quirky treasures.

While sitting by the garden one evening, a soft wind hinted at a change. The stars twinkled a bit brighter. It felt like the universe was sharing a secret with Aditya.

Curiosity led him to explore new places on the outskirts of town. Lush forests unfolded, streams whispered, and birds sang melodies that echoed ancient stories. In a hidden cave, Aditya found a mural depicting the journey of life. It connected him to the universe in a way he hadn't felt before.

Returning to the town square, the animals gathered, sensing the newfound energy. Under the glittering night sky, Aditya felt a deep connection to everything around him.

And so, Aditya's story in the quiet town continued a simple tale of self-discovery, friendship with animals, and a silent celebration of the beauty in everyday moments. Each day unfolded like a page in a cosmic diary, where the wonders of existence spoke in the shared silence of a world finding its rhythm.

FIVE

AN UNEXPECTED TURN

One bright morning, as Aditya explored a corner of the town he hadn't visited before, he stumbled upon a small playground. Swings swayed gently, and an abandoned sandbox waited for playful hands. To his surprise, he noticed a little girl sitting on a bench, her eyes wide with curiosity.

"Hey there," Aditya greeted with a warm smile. The little girl looked up, her face lighting up with surprise and joy. It seemed like she had been exploring this quiet town on her own.

"What's your name?" Aditya asked, sitting down beside her.

"I'm Mia," she replied, a hint of shyness in her voice.

Aditya shared his own name and explained how he had found himself in this silent world. Mia listened with wide-eyed wonder, and as he spoke, the animals gathered around, as if welcoming a new member to their community.

Aditya's routine took on a different hue with Mia by his side. They explored together, discovering hidden nooks and crannies of the town. The animals, accustomed to Aditya, accepted Mia with open curiosity. Dogs wagged their tails, cats purred, and the raccoon, ever mischievous, brought a small flower as a gift.

The playground became a lively spot once again. Aditya and Mia swung on the swings, built sandcastles, and played games with the animals, joining in the fun. Laughter, absent for so long in this quiet town, echoed through the air.

As days turned into weeks, Aditya and Mia shared stories of the world they came from, the people they missed, and the simple joys they found in this newfound companionship. They painted and read books from the forgotten bookstore, and Mia even tried her hand at playing the piano. One evening, as they sat by the garden, watching the sunset paint the sky in warm hues, Mia spoke, "Do you think there are more people out there like us?"

Aditya pondered the question, looking at the animals and the quiet town. "Maybe," he said, "but we have each other and this incredible world for now. "The stars above sparkled, seemingly affirming their shared sentiment. Aditya, Mia, and their animal friends continued to write the story of the quiet town tale of unexpected friendships, shared adventures, and the simplicity of joy found in the company of one another.

SIX
MYSTERY.

Me: This is all strange Mia!

Mia. What? My **Paneer sandwich**?

Me. What? No. Wait, did you say paneer sandwich?

Mia. Yep.

Me. May I have some?

Mia. Yep.

Me. Thanks.

If you don't know, I was looking for people. I had questions in my mind. Where did they go? Why did they go? Are there any other people left in this town? These questions floated around my head rent free. I wish there was a helmet to answer these questions, like the hermit in the Honeycomb textbook. At school. Sigh. Wait a minute. No school?

Yeah! *Me doing my happy dance*

Of Course that went on till Mia gave her what the what look. I stopped eventually as I was embarrassed.

Mia. What was all that about?

Me. Nothing. I just realized that when you're the only person left on the earth (Or maybe India) means no school.

Mia. Really. Do you seriously realize that now?

Me: Yeah, um. **YEAH**

It's OK. Hey, did you notice the whole world is missing except their pets, so might as well bring them to the shed.

Me. Mm-hmm. * Nodding. *

OK, so. Task #5 Find all the pets in the city and protect them. Wait. Since all the people are missing one, the wild animals come out and gobble us up. Gulp (Not about the animals I was just thinking...).

SEVEN
NEEDS AND FEEDS

Man, yesterday was rough. Mia is not some 10-year-old girl who I found the street. She was like some survival expert, a hunter, has a heart of spirit, all that.

But now here I am at the grocery store. Grabbing all medical supplies, food, snacks, and. Um. Toys of the soft kind Hehe.

Wait for Ohm. Bingo!!!! I grabbed all the Flavors of all kinds. Good God, they're not perishable food. They'll last us for months!

But since there were no more people, all Wi-Fi to me. Don't ask me how, I guess I was just lucky. Anyway, I learned how to cook chips, fries, omelets, paneer, and best of all, and most importantly, some nice and soft rice! OH, we are crushing this! What, do we say hmm oh yeah "THE SURVIVAL PLAGUE" (Gosh! that's a Terrible name)

I soon reached our house. Mia was right there on the sofa playing the piano. I silently walked by and envied her (I always wanted to learn how to play the piano).

Me. Hi, Mia.

Mia. Hi, good morning. Have you got all the supplies?

Me. Yes, yes, I did.

Mia. What's up? Anything on your mind?

Me. Nah, nothing.

Mia. OK? Any peers? Right prepared Breakfast. It's on the table.

Man, it seems I can't share anything with anybody in this world. Except for the animals. I walked up to the table and found a record player beside my sandwich. I tried to play the record player. But to no avail. Turns out. I did not bring CDs for it yet.

EIGHT

WHAT A PET GETS

Me: Guess whose birthday is today? It's catnip! Yippee!

Mia: OK, so um. Balloons? Check. Cat food? Check. Premium cat food? Check. Guests Check. Dog food? Check. Grass. Check. OK. I think we are all ready for the party. Aditya. Do you have the cake?

Me: Yes, I do. I'll keep it right on the table. OH wait, here he comes quick. Hide!

All: Surprise! Mooo! (that was not me...that was the cow...)

Yesterday, we partied hard until the lights went out, as the power had gone out temporarily. The animals freaked out. We comforted them and fed them. The cows got their fresh grass, the horse ate the candle, the sheep licked the floor's frosting, and the dog had a quality pedigree. And catnip had its favorite pickle mixed with curd rice.

Me and Mia were so tired that we directly went to bed.

In the morning 8: 04 AM.

OK, something weird happened here. Me and Mia woke up to an eerie silence again. No snores, no cat, no animals, and the door was open. Shoot.

We searched the shed only to find Bessie the cow. We had a feeling If Bessie was here, then the animals must be at the river. Bessie hated the river, so she stayed back.

We reached the river. Turns out. Our search was fruitful! Our assumptions were right! They were all at the river, splashing water everywhere.

When did they become independent? But after seeing how happy they were. They had no heart to scold them. After all, they are safe and that's what matters.

So, Mia clattered off to get Bessie in the meantime. I'll super-supervise the animals. Of course, I can't risk anybody wandering off to the forest again.

The last time we were at the river, our beloved dog Doggone somehow slipped out of our sight and somehow managed to get lost in a forest.

Man, imagine how peaceful it was at home when it was not alone. Again, that much. But a farm is much better than a home. In fact, I might as well say farming is better than school. I used to have fears that if I did not study, I might end up inside of a trash can! But turns out I was wrong. I had nothing to worry about. In fact, I never felt so alive in years.

And the best part is, when you are alone, money does not matter anymore. All you can do is stretch your legs, arms, bones and do whatever you want. You and I can feel my legs, arms, and bones. Rather than being a mindless zombie. Playing a video game and being stuck to the chair but standing, plucking crops, feeding the animals. Getting groceries is something I haven't done in years. Or maybe I never even done it.

NINE

DUST-TOP

All right, so it has been an entire month since I touched my laptop (which I did not take from the abandoned tech store). I probably must check on it. It might have caught so much dust since I was away.

It was raining aggressively for two days. The animals are locked up in the shed with Mia and Laila. If you don't know, me and Mia were walking our dogs when we heard....an empty, faint cry, we rushed to the source of the sound to find a six-year-old girl, bruised. We immediately gave her attention and now she stays with us. Since then, the girls had been talking like chatterboxes all day long.

I just realized somebody needed help in running the Wi-Fi towers for ages. OK, no, not ages, months. I thought I could help but I don't know many computers or WIFI towers anyway....

Anyways, turns out there are more people who are adults looking for other people here and everywhere. They post stuff on YouTube, Facebook, and Instagram just to find the people of their land.

Ding Dong!

Huh. It must be the girls.

But when I opened the door, there were no girls, instead a middle-aged woman looking for shelter. I agreed immediately because I was starting to feel lonely.

She asked about my parent's whereabouts, to which I answered. I don't have any parents. I'm a 13-year-old orphan boy living with a helpful 10-year-old and raising a ...... Never mind.

Well, what are your names? She asked nicely.

I'm Aditya, the oldest child. My friend Mia is the middle child and Lyla is the youngest child.

I was so engrossed in our conversation that I did not notice the girls slip in. But after a while, I found myself out of the next conversation between the girls and the lady. Man being the only boy stinks. It stinks really bad. Now I'm starting to think I might need a bath.

I guess I'll just shove it off to take my mind off for a bit.

Before I went to take a bath, I just questioned myself. I thought, where are the people? Are there only a few people left in the world? Or are they? Do some robots? Are AI people left behind? Yes, AI. Because now robots exist. They finally figured it out. Now they rule most of the companies. I guess there was one that was running the Wi-Fi towers. Don't worry, I don't think it's some robot invasion or something. I just want the robots to be friendly. Or even better, the robots are humans!

TEN

LOOK OUT!1!!11!

OH no. My worst nightmares came true! I just saw a dude post on YouTube a live video of a cheetah or leopard. Can't tell the difference, but they were running around town. I think we should lock the shed. And the house right away.

The worst part is the girls were outside plucking berries. I ran to them and warned them about the cheetah. But it is looked at my face and laughed historically. What are these people? Are they mad!?

I explained this is a bad thing. You know, without much human syllabus, and civilization around, the cities became animal playgrounds! Our houses are restaurants, and the shed is the…. **GULP**. Edible toys!

But the lady calmly explained that there was no cheetah or leopard on the loose, it was just some poorly edited video. Plus, if someone were to record, they would do it in distance or out of a security Camera. Nobody's brave enough to approach the cheetah up close. Plus, the cheetah would smell the scent of the human anyway and would chase It whatever the scent is. Aditya, you're safe. There is nothing to worry about. As you know now it's the month of April and you know that the 1st of April is April Fool's Day doesn't mean that. The rest of the month won't be a full month. You have to be careful about anything they post about on the Internet. Even the girls this morning doubted their choices on Plucking berries today. You're not the only one who is scared by the Internet. But you have to investigate the proof. Where is the cheetah? Why is there a cheetah? If you don't, you'll just end up sitting in your house all day thinking, when's the cheetah going to roam and pass by their house?

Man, what a huge relief. What a wild lookout. Better be careful!

Honestly, it's annoying to think that people are now playing a prank on another level that there are no police officers to arrest them.

ELEVEN

FLASH BACK

Oh man, Oh man. Oh, man! Just one day for the match exam! This is not enough! Why? What's wrong? What's wrong, Aditya? What's wrong?

Aditya yo buddy, what's wrong? Why are you tense?

Just look at our math syllabus. It just says everything in the textbook. How are we supposed to study everything in the textbook in just three days!?

Dude, chill out. Yikes.

Just do your best, revise what's important and I'm sure you will complete the syllabus and score well in maths. It's not like It's not like this, anybody who asks you to be perfect in life, otherwise you'll be kicked out of the village or something. It's just an exam so just prepare accordingly and I'm sure you will get amazing results. You may even surprise yourself.

End of flashback.

Man, if there was still school it would have been bad. Good thing it is extinct!

OK, time to get my work done. In order my Do List cannot complete itself.

#1 Collect eggs from the shed.

#2 Clean the shed.

#3 Clean the house.

#4 Walk the dog.

Total 4 tasks. That may sound easy but quite difficult. Getting eggs from Mike the chicken is like a battle between Rama and Ravana!

And cleaning the shed isn't easy at all! I would clean it, it'll be clean for a time then all of a sudden it'll get dirty in just about a month. There is grass everywhere and dusting every nook Is painful. Luckily, I'm not cleaning the animals or their fences.

The worst part about being alone? You still have to do chores even when there's nobody to instruct you to do so. Sometimes life is just unfair.

While I was cleaning, Mia was milking the cows, the lad was cooking breakfast at the house and Lyla was sleeping.

Breakfast!

The lady made us delicious Idli and peanut chutney.

We ate the food with relish and continued our work months ago in January or July. I used to have a body looking for comfort for months. But after loads of work and hiking, what I had to do now made me healthier and stronger. This strange pandemic kind of benefited everyone in every way. Good thing I'm not entirely alone. There are at least a few numbers of people left in the world! Well, things may get better or worse on the other end so maybe just go slow.

TWELVE
DIARY THEIF

RECORDING KSSS KSSS** This is Aditya with you and KSS today we are gonna take a look at KSS Mia's diary- OO- LA-LA-LA Facts! Let's see hmmm. ***reading

1. Earth is the third planet from the Sun, with an equatorial circumference of about 40,075 kilometers.
2. The highest point on Earth is Mount Everest, while the Challenger Deep in the Mariana Trench is the lowest point.
3. Earth's atmosphere is mainly composed of nitrogen (78%) and

.... There are more than 100 facts in Mia's diary but I'm no longer interested

Oh the strange lady has a diary too! And there is a poem

Cats roam silent in the night,
Whiskers twitch in soft moonlight.
No loud barks, just purrs so right.
Eyes gleam with a golden hue,
Purring whispers, calming too.
No chaos, just a tranquil view.

Soft fur invites a gentle touch,
Moonlit dreams that cats clutch.
No disruptions, just a quiet hush.
Curled up in a circle tight,
Tails wrapped in the pale moonlight.
No disturbances, just pure delight.
A feline grace, a calming trend,
In silence, cats become friends.
No clamor, just peace to lend.
blah blah blah.....

welp, not a surprise that she likes cats.. Ok here is Mia's blue diary...

More facts ***sigh*** and is that Baby Mia-

MIA: Ahem!

Aditya: Uh-oh

MIA: AAADITYAAAA!

Well. We'll see Aditya with Brocken bones next time!

THIRTEEN
CHAPTER 1

Aditya, Mia, and Lyla decide to move to a new place near the river. Now the mysterious lady, Kattie resides at their old house. They were running low on supplies and needed rations so they set out to the city for more supplies. Aditya suddenly runs into some familiar faces.

"Hey! Is that who I think it is." I said gleefully.

It was his old friend Mahesh and his younger brother Mukesh! What were they doing there?

"OH MY GOD! HI ADITYA! It's been a long-time man!" exclaimed Mahesh

"Glad to know that you too are not one of the people who suddenly disappear off the face of the Earth, we finally met friend."

said Mahesh as he shook hands with Me.

It felt so good. We met after a long time!

I was so excited that I immediately started interrogating him about his background.

"Where do you live?"

"Any other Friends?"

"Any pets?"

"Why did you come here?"

"Can you come with and live with us? We have a whole countryside to ourselves!!!"

Mahesh did not bother to answer the previous ones but he was interested in living with me, so he and his brother decided to move to my house.

Mia and Lyla have their own house together, so why not? They have the whole countryside to themselves so, who will Tax them?

Mukesh was hesitant at first but decided to do the same.

Mahesh sure did change! A year ago, he was the weakest in our class, and look at him now! He is now tall! Taller than me! I was so surprised, that I wanted to ask his secret. Maybe not now but later.

As we were walking, It started to rain. We arrived soaking wet. Our clothes were dripping, our hair was fresh out of the sauna.

For the next few minutes, we all dried ourselves. Mia offered to cook dinner. I did not refuse! I almost feel bad for our guest (Mahesh and his brother). It is their first evening here and they already caught a cold.

"Dinner is ready," said Mia.

We all waited patiently for our warm soup. Say, I always wondered when Mia got the time to cook.

FOURTEEN

CHAPTER 2

Now, Reunions are fun, but priorities are important. So, Aditya and his companions, Mahesh and Mukesh decide to visit the nearby grocery to get supplies. It was clear the storm might arrive soon. But Aditya and Mahesh had other plans...

"Hey, Aditya." Said Mahesh, with a little smirk on his face.

"Yeah, Mahesh?"

"I want to scare my brother today! And I know exactly how to do it!"

I was taken aback, I was hesitant at first, but who wouldn't want a good laugh? I'm sure nothing bad will come out of this.

We all reached the store. It was slightly dark and was in a bad state.

Mukesh was a little scared, but he went ahead once we encouraged him to get us some juice. PERFECT!

Me and Mahesh hid behind some trees. We waited for Mukesh to come out of the store searching for us. For a while, we were hiding but Mukesh is yet to turn up.

"Hey, where is Mukesh? Shouldn't he have found us by now?"

I asked.

Suddenly, we heard a huge crashing sound. What was that? We came running into the store, a little worried about Mukesh.

"Mukesh! Mukesh?" We yelled.

But there was no response. What if he ran home through a gapping gash on that wall? Maybe he is home, right? We called Mia and Lyla, hoping they would bring us good news.

"Hello? Mia?"

"Yes, who is this?"

"It is me, Aditya!"

"ADITYA HOW MANY TIMES I HAVE TOLD YOU NOT TO FORGET YOUR PHONE I-"

"Yeah, Yeah, I'm sorry! Listen! Did you see Mukesh coming home?"

"No? We did not, what happened?"

"Mukesh......err......he uh I don't know how to say this but, he is uhm missing..."

CALL ENDED

Meanwhile....

Mukesh soon finds out the cause of the teleportation He is so frustrated that he throws the ball, and it cracks, and out comes a strange gas.

"Why do I even bother? THEY ALWAYS GET ME INTO TROUBLE" said Mukesh, in anger.

"Oh, how I hate thrift stores and its aisles... I hate them! And as for this STUPID ball!"

Throws the sphere

"Huh!? What is happening now!"

The gas comes out of the sphere. It is green and out comes a table with scrolls.

"Woah What are these? Scrolls?"

Suddenly a strange voice started to address him

"THEY ARE SCROLLS OF FATE CHILD"
"What the-AAAHHHH"

FIFTEEN

CHAPTER 3

She.... Did she just cut the call? I don't understand why she cut the call.

Suddenly, the doors threw open. Mia walked in saying "Can't you do a simple job?! I have been expecting better than this! How did you lose Mukesh? What happened here?"

"We just wanted to prank him! For a while, we hid, but Mukesh never came outside, and neither did we hear anything. When we went inside, he was gone, just like that!"I explained.

I am so scared........and shocked! I feel so bad for doing this!

Mahesh is heartbroken, he thought of his brother as an annoyance but now their being separated with no clue on where he is the end of the world for him.

Just then Lyla suggested,

"Instead of fighting, let's check the security cameras?"

"It's not possible. This building is a year old now, and the computer must have died down by now," said Mia.

"Well, there goes that idea-"

"Wait! I can fix a computer! My dad was a technician and I have seen him work before! Let me try!" exclaimed

Mahesh.

"It was a bit of a hustle but I guess that fixes it," said Mahesh.

"That's one way of fixing the computer I guess..." said Lyla, a tad bit impressed.

"Come on! Time is of the essence, let's now see the camera!" exclaimed Mia.

(ALL) WOAH!

SIXTEEN

CHAPTER 4

You read it when it comes ut. K byeee! :)

Hello And Good Bye-see-you-next-time

Hi everybody, I am Rohan the definite author of this book! I really like stories and writing them is pure joy! So why not share it with you?

I will keep writing for you and entertainment. See you next time, and keep chugging water!